This brand-new project
aims to encourage boys and girls
between the ages of seven and twelve to
be "emotional explorers," people who work in
a responsible and decisive way to become more
attuned to their emotional lives, leave a better world
for those following them, and help those around them
to grow.

The book is an invitation to reflection, debate, creativity,
and the sharing of experiences that allow us to take
action to improve ourselves. Only if we are aware that
something is valuable will we protect it, care for it,
respect it, and get it to grow.

**We hope you enjoy this innovative
proposal and set off on an exciting
inner and external adventure!**

To Zulma and the whole
generation of CAPA children

HOW DOES THIS BOOK WORK?

The contents of this book are very open, leaving space for teachers to enrich it by developing the activities and ideas to their taste.

Each of the five chapters has the same structure:

It starts with a double-page illustration and three questions. The ideas the illustrations suggest will start the debate about the theme. This page helps break the ice and invites children to "see" and "read" beyond what is shown on the page.

Chapter 1 introduces the parallel nature of our outer and inner worlds. Through a vocabulary and images reflecting

what we are calling "environmental ecology," this double page introduces the idea of emotional ecology and helps us understand what happens inside us, what causes it, and what consequences it has.

Environmental and emotional education are discussed as parallel ideas. One concept supports the other, enriches it, and enables us to develop and understand it better.

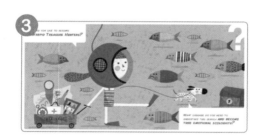

Once we have identified what happens inside us and its consequences, **the third double page urges children to think** about how they can begin to act in a different and better-adjusted way. The big illustration again becomes an invitation to participate, and the questions stimulate a discussion of

possible solutions and tools that will help us achieve our objective.

Through the six proposals in each chapter (as an activity, story, narrative, game, or situation), **we work on each of the skills needed to solve the obstacles identified,** strengthening ourselves and helping us become emotionally ecological people.

Each proposal has a small guide for teachers, who are encouraged to adapt the ideas and activities to the group or the question being worked on.

Each proposal has the same structure and involves four distinct parts: the objective, an explanation of the proposal, reflections on the proposal, and conclusions that can be drawn.

Without further ado, we invite you to travel into your emotional landscapes, to conquer lands, overcome your dragons, search for treasure and find it, and, above all, to protect the most valuable thing we have, our diversity.

SUMMARY

TWO WORLDS TO CARE FOR

?

- Do you know what **THE WORD "ECO" MEANS?**
- Have you ever thought that we all have at least **TWO HOMES TO LOOK AFTER?** **WHAT ARE THEY?**
- What do you think **AN "EMOTIONAL ECOLOGIST"** might be like?

5

We form part of an ecosystem involving a great WHOLE: the universe. We live on a small planet, Earth, the third in the solar system. The Earth is a privileged planet, as it has the essential conditions to support life: a mean temperature of about 59ºF, water in liquid form, and an atmosphere heavy with oxygen. We share it with other human beings, plants, and animals. The Earth is our external home. We have no other and we must take care of it.

Let's think...

- Have you ever searched the Internet for images of the Earth from space? Why is the Earth called the blue planet?

- In what zone of the Earth do you live? Is it cold or hot? Does it rain a lot? Are there long hours of sunshine or is it usually cloudy?

- Have you heard of the Earth's force of gravity? Do you know that this is a result of a magnetic nucleus inside it that attracts everything on the surface?

- What else do you know about your external home? What would you like to explore?

- How many years have you spent on Earth? Do you know that our oldest ancestors were living on it more than 250,000 years ago?

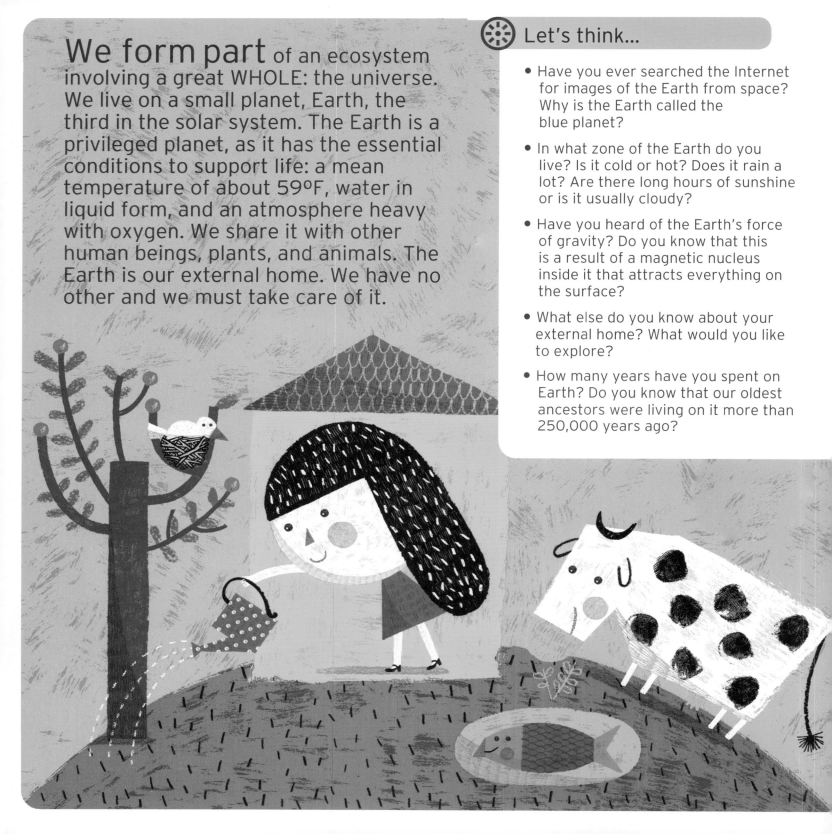

Our inner self is like the planet Earth. It is an ecosystem in itself, with its own sources of energy, natural resources, systems of protection and repair, and foods. It is a planet full of light and dark, agreeable and disagreeable, emotional colors, a planet full of landscapes we all know and many more still to be discovered. It has a changing climate: storms and rain, sunny days, cloudy days, starry nights, varying moons. Don't you think it is worth discovering and looking after such a fascinating planet?

Let's think...

- What do you know of your inner planet?
- Do you like what you see?
- Are there areas you still haven't visited?
- How do you think it protects, repairs, and feeds itself?
- Have you ever felt the great strength you have inside you?
- Do you agree that your inner self contains many treasures to be discovered?

WHAT LUGGAGE DO YOU NEED TO UNDERTAKE THIS SEARCH **AND BECOME TRUE EMOTIONAL ECOLOGISTS?**

THE PLANET "SOMEWHERE"

⊛ Objective:

To realize that, when everything is changing or something goes wrong in the external world, we can search for tranquility inside ourselves.

Story:

Many years ago a planet was born. Its name was Somewhere and it had a lot of problems: it suffered earthquakes and hurricanes, and erupting volcanoes were continually re-forming its geography. With so much change occurring, Somewhere no longer knew who it was, which saddened it. Just to survive was an endless struggle. What could Somewhere do? In desperation, it looked inside and examined itself as it had never done before. Somewhere discovered unknown parts such as layers of black coal, oil deposits, and seams of gold, silver, and precious stones – and below all this, a stable and heavy region that not even the most furious storm could move, push, or deform. It was a powerful magnet, full of energy. Somewhere had never seen this part of itself.

"Who are you?" it asked.

"I'm your core. I had no voice until you found me. Now you know you're not alone. I am your strength and your center. I keep you stable in your solar system. Now that we know each other, together we can improve our planet."

This is how Somewhere found happiness and learned to value the treasures of its planet.

⊛ Reflections on the story

- Why do you think Somewhere was sad?
- What were its main problems?
- What happened when, instead of looking only toward the outside, Somewhere looked inside itself?
- What riches did it discover?
- If you look inside yourself, what treasures can you find?
- How do you feel when you trust yourself?

⊛ Conclusions for further work

We have two options in life: we can live focused on all the bad things that happen to us, or search for answers inside ourselves to solve these problems. If we opt for the former, we will often feel like Somewhere, always fighting to survive and not in control of what happens to us. Instead, if we look inside ourselves, we will feel that we are holding the reins of our life.

If we devote time to discovering our inner treasure, we will feel more confident and brave when difficulties arise.

OUR EMOTIONAL SOLAR SYSTEM

Objective:

To realize that we are diverse; each of us is unique and all of us together form a system in which we orbit around the sun of love.

Activity:

You will need white Styrofoam balls of different sizes (one for each child), paints, colored paper, glue, a fishing line, a hoop, and scissors.

Each child chooses a ball that will represent him or her. The child has to think what kind of planet it is, how big it is, what color it is, and what characteristic makes it special. Then each child designs the planet. Once finished, the children present their planet to the group, and the planets are hung with fishing line on a hoop to represent the emotional solar system of the group. The teacher will have prepared a big ball with the words "The Sun of Love," which will be placed in the center of the hoop.

After each presentation, the children share what they like most about the planet of their companion.

Reflections on the activity

- What three words would you use to define your planet?
- What do you like most about it?
- What place does it occupy in the classroom's solar system?
- What would you like to improve on your planet?
- What can you do to achieve this?

Conclusions for further work

We are unique and different. There are no better or worse planets. They all have their strong points and ways they can be improved.

Diversity is a source of wealth and beauty. It is important to observe others and assess their qualities, as we can all learn from each other. We just have to pay attention to each other.

Telling others what we like about them is a source of gratitude and love. It improves the emotional climate and brings us happiness.

11

MY FAMILY GALAXY

✿ Objective:

To be aware that we are part of a family in which everyone has a place, a function, something to contribute, and a way of being and behaving. To reflect on the people closest to us: who are they and what they are like.

Activity:

Each child needs crayons and a big piece of paper or poster board.

Each child is given a piece of paper and asked to draw a circle in the middle with his or her name inside. They then will draw various concentric orbits, emulating a solar system, with their circle at its center.

Next, the children will make a list of everyone in their immediate family and draw a planet for each of them, paint it, and place it in one of the orbits they drew.

When the children are finished, their papers are hung on the wall and each child explains what his or her family galaxy is like.

✿ Reflections on the Activity

- In what order have you placed the various members of your family?

- Why are some in close orbit, and why are others more distant?

- Is anyone in your family missing?

- What size is each planet? Are there some bigger planets and smaller planets, or are they all the same size?

- Does the color of the planet have any significance? Does it refer to a particular characteristic of the person, and if so, what?

✿ Conclusions for further work

Around us are people with whom we share our lives. Some are closer to us, to our heart, and others are farther away, or at least that's what we feel. However, this feeling is not permanent, and may change throughout our lives. For example, people who previously seemed distant may become much closer to us, and the opposite may occur.

Together we are stronger, but it is important to know how to maintain the right distance from each other and to stay in our orbit, as the planets do. If we do this, we will avoid colliding with each other.

MY PART OF THE COLLAGE

Objective:

To learn to introduce ourselves to a group and identify a rich, new vision of ourselves.

Activity:

Make a collage using colorful images, words, and phrases taken from magazines, newspapers, postcards, posters – anything that might refer to emotions, values, or beliefs.

Groups of four to six children are asked to form a circle. Each group is given scissors and a collection of images and words to choose from. They are asked to remain silent throughout the activity. While background music is playing, the members of each group pass around the materials. The children choose the piece that best represents them or that they are drawn to, and cut it out.

When everyone has their piece cut out, the music stops and the presentations begin. Each child stands up, looks at the rest of the group, and introduces him/herself, saying: "I am ... and I have chosen this piece because ... "

To extend the activity and look at it from another point of view, the pieces can be mixed together after the presentations, and each child chooses one at random, looks for the person with whom it corresponds, and presents it instead of that person.

Reflections on the activity

- Did you really choose the piece that you think suited you best, or simply the one you liked the most?

- How did you feel while you waited for your turn?

- Did someone else get the piece you wanted for yourself?

- Would you know how to put your piece back onto the material it was cut from? Did you notice if it was at the top, bottom, or at the side?

- Did you see what words or drawings surrounded the piece you chose?

- What did you learn from this group activity?

Conclusions for further work

Although we don't get to choose many of our characteristics, it is important to understand them, know how to value them, and get the maximum benefit out of them.

Often we don't look closely at our surroundings, but it is important that we do so, since we form part of an ALL in which we are unique pieces. If we don't occupy our place in this ALL, we will leave an empty space that no one else can fill.

13

THE BAGGAGE OF THE EMOTIONAL ECOLOGIST

Objective:

To learn to choose what baggage to carry in life, and what to let go of. To figure out what helps us versus what weighs us down and is no use for anything. Starting with this awareness, we will be ready to set out on the exciting journey of LIVING.

Activity:

Each member of the group is asked to draw a big suitcase or backpack that contains all the items on the list below, and which they will need to set out on the exciting journey through life. The children are asked to imagine what each of these things represents and to think where to put them in the suitcase, depending on their use or importance.

List:

1. A magnifying scanner to know at all times what emotions you feel. These emotions will indicate whether you're on the right path or not.
2. An umbrella of good self-esteem to ride through the storms of insults, difficulties, and pollution of all kinds.
3. A pot of good-times jam, to remember them when the going gets tough.
4. Emotional vitamins of caresses, embraces, kisses, and smiles.
5. Music, songs, stories, and tales to feed the soul.
6. A magic kite that will allow you to fly wherever you want by dressing you in four characteristics – creativity, love, peace, and autonomy (CLAPA).
7. A drawbridge you can let down to communicate with others, even at difficult moments.
8. A box filled with emotions of every kind and color, used to paint all the landscapes you visit.
9. A virtual mental trainer to improve everyday ideas, thoughts, criteria, determination, and all the skills of a good explorer.
10. A compass of values that show the good path of life.
11. Something you can invent.

Reflections on the activity

- What did you add to your list?
- Would you take anything else on your journey through life?
- Is there something you're carrying in your baggage now that you think is unnecessary and just gets in the way?
- What things in your baggage do you consider essential and basic?
- In what different ways did your companions imagine their list?

Conclusions for further work

Sometimes we carry with us useless materials that weigh us down a lot: insults, fears that block our reactions, thoughts that crush us, insecurities, guilt, etc. It is important to unload these stones so our journey is neither slow nor disagreeable.

In reality, we only possess what we cannot lose in a shipwreck: qualities, skills, knowledge, abilities, feelings, imagination . . .

We can never lose what we are, and no one can take these things away from us. It is smart to acquire this sort of baggage.

TAKING CARE OF MY HOUSES

⚙ Objective:

To become aware that every house needs upkeep and care if we want to lead a good life in it. To learn to compare the needs of our external and internal houses and decide what we can do to improve their quality.

Activity:

We will need a large piece of wrapping paper, red and green sticky notes, and something to write with.

The entire group makes a mural with wrapping paper, on which three large items are painted: the planet Earth, a house, and a person.

Fifteen green and fifteen red sticky notes are given to each child (five per area) and they are asked the following questions:

What problems or break-downs could there be *on the Earth, in my house, and in myself* that have to be prevented or repaired?

Each child reflects on the question and writes down the problems that come to mind on the red sticky notes.

What can I do or what should I look after *on the Earth, in my house, and in myself* to make everything work properly?

Each child reflects on the question and writes down the problems that come to mind on the green sticky notes.

⚙ Reflections on the activity

- Do you feel responsible for what the world in which you live is like? Are you part of its problems or are you a part of the solution? Do you create or destroy?

- What responsibilities do each of you have in the house you live in and share? Do you expect someone else to make sure everything is running smoothly? What contributions do you make? Do they help to create balance or create problems?

- Are you responsible for the person you are becoming? Do you like the way you are? Is there something you'd like to improve? Do you look for guilty parties outside yourself when something goes wrong, or do you try to change what doesn't work?

⚙ Conclusions for further work

Earth's problems are pretty similar to the problems that our house or we ourselves might have: dirt, things that don't work as well as they should, break-downs, illnesses, injustice, abandonment, scarce resources, etc.

If we improve ourselves, our house will improve and, all together, we will improve the Earth.

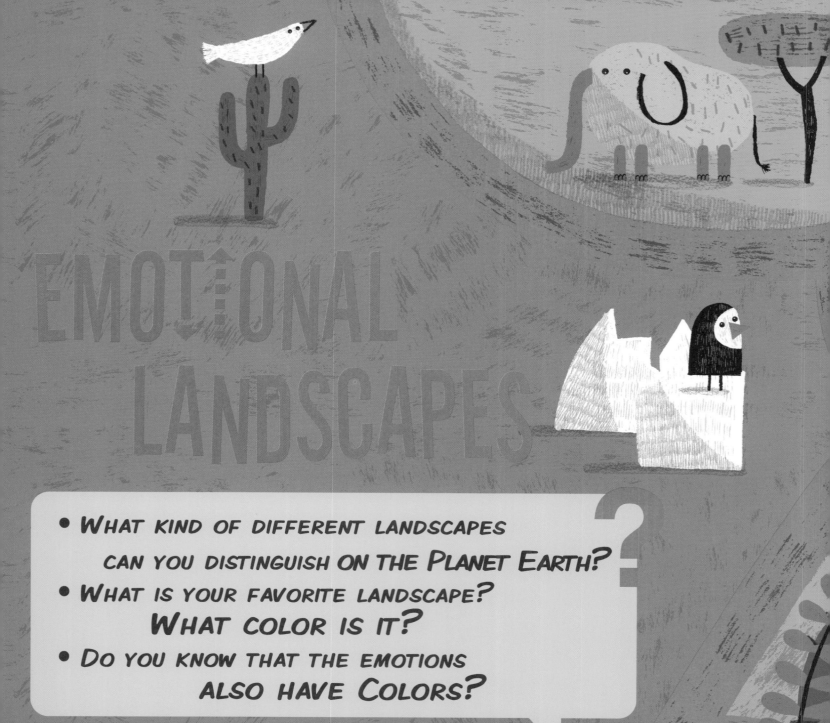

EMOTIONAL LANDSCAPES

- **WHAT KIND OF DIFFERENT LANDSCAPES CAN YOU DISTINGUISH ON THE PLANET EARTH?**
- **WHAT IS YOUR FAVORITE LANDSCAPE? WHAT COLOR IS IT?**
- **DO YOU KNOW THAT THE EMOTIONS ALSO HAVE COLORS?**

Did you know that 71 percent of the Earth is water and only 29 percent is solid land? And that much of this 29 percent is covered by snow? Other parts are mountains, deserts, and fertile lands suitable for cultivation.

The Earth contains highly diverse landscapes and living beings that live in every area of our planet, from the coldest zones where the ice never disappears to the baking deserts. Heat, intense cold, water scarcity, and lack of vegetation do not impede life. Living beings are capable of adapting themselves to the most adverse surroundings: for example, polar bears and penguins in icy regions; camels and dromedaries in the desert; and pigeons, sparrows, and rats in polluted cities.

⚘ Let's think...

- **Guess...**

  What do you call the landscape of a place where the sky is clear and cloudless, where only the sound of the wind is heard, it rains very little, and it is extremely hot during the day and intensely cold at night? Do you think there are people who live in a place like this?

- **Guess...**

  In what landscape with very fertile soil do a great many tall trees grow, as well as beautifully colored plants and flowers, with all kinds of animals, abundant insects, and butterflies hidden in the thick vegetation?

  Is there anywhere like this in your country?

We can compare the varying feelings and emotional situations we experience with a particular kind of landscape. Here are some examples:

- Deserts of loneliness: moments when we feel abandoned or when it is hard to communicate with others.

- Plains and meadows of flowers: when we feel well, tranquil, calm, when things are going well and aren't too difficult.

- Arid, mountainous landscapes: when we have a problem to solve or we have to make an effort to get what we want. Facing such a challenge, we can feel tired and dispirited, or brave and strong enough to reach the peak.

- Seascapes: moments of relaxation and calm.

- Marshy areas: situations that smell bad, encountering lies and evil.

We have an inner world full of landscapes painted with highly differing emotions: joy, gratitude, love, friendship, sadness, fear, anger, hope. Do you feel like exploring it?

 Let's think...

- Is the landscape you see and feel the same landscape that people beside you see and feel?

- Is it possible that, where one person sees a precipice, another sees a bridge?

- Why do you think this happens to us?

WHAT DIFFERENT KINDS OF LANDSCAPES HAVE YOU KNOWN, AND **WHAT DID YOU FEEL IN EACH OF THEM?**

RIGHT NOW, WHAT IS
YOUR INNER LANDSCAPE?

MY EMOTIONAL LANDSCAPES

⚙ Objective:

To connect with our emotions and relate them to a particular landscape. To understand that the same landscape may mean different things to different people.

Activity:

Make a mural relating emotions to landscapes.

Each child is given a list of different emotions, along with various magazines. They are asked to look in the magazines for a landscape that represents each emotion, cut it out, and make a mural out of all the images, writing down the emotion beside the landscape chosen. At the end, all the murals will be hung on the wall and, in silence and with soft background music, everyone will look at the murals.

Each participant will write down the name of the person he or she identifies with most in illustrating a particular emotion.

Groups are formed on the basis of these similarities, and each group discusses for ten minutes why they chose each landscape to represent a particular emotion.

List of emotions: sadness, anger, joy, fear, love, peace, loneliness, happiness.

⚙ Reflections on the activity

- Do you think it is possible to feel all the emotions on the list at the same time?

- Have you ever felt several emotions at the same time? When?

- Why do you think one landscape can represent different emotions?

- What can you do to better understand what others feel?

⚙ Conclusions for further work

Landscapes are the metaphor for the various situations we experience. Our emotions are its colors.

Our emotions have different nuances and degrees of intensity. Just as many colors can be created from the primary colors, we rarely experience just one single, pure emotion.

All "landscapes" have their charm and reason for existence, and we can find beauty and learn new things in even the toughest landscapes. Just as only seeing one landscape would mean a loss of richness and diversity, we lose richness by closing ourselves off to the range of our emotions.

EXCURSION INTO THE DESERT

⚙ Objective:
To learn to identify what is necessary and what is superfluous at difficult moments or in tough situations.

Activity:
Teams of three to six people are formed to organize an expedition into the desert. Each team must agree on a single list of items to take along:

1. As you will have to carry your luggage, what will you take?

2. Of all the items you have mentioned, which ones are indispensable? You're only allowed to take ten.

3. If, in addition to everything you have chosen, you could carry five more qualities, which of the following would you choose: will, courage, joy, perseverance, self-control, good spirits, patience, calm, resignation, strength, intelligence, decisiveness, speed?

4. What kind of companion would you want to have on this expedition across the desert? Describe the person, indicating five personal characteristics that you think the companion should have. What three characteristics should the person not have?

⚙ Reflections on the activity

- What has been the most difficult situation you have experienced over a period of time? How did you feel at the worst moment? What or who helped you to overcome it?

- What personal characteristics helped you to get out of this difficult situation?

- What's the most important thing you learned from the experience?

- How important are the people beside you when the going gets tough?

- Of the qualities the group has chosen, which ones do you have? Which ones could you improve?

⚙ Conclusions for further work

When difficult situations (deserts) occur, we get angry; we protest and rebel.

When you cross an emotional desert, you don't want a companion who is pushing you or makes decisions without thinking of you. You want to face the difficulties together and encourage each other.

The relationship with the people we love takes on new value in difficult times.

Even in the desert there is life. In crisis situations, it is possible to grow and improve. Good emotional luggage will make the difference.

23

WHICH KING OF THE JUNGLE ARE YOU?

✺ Objective:

To reflect on the various attitudes we may adopt in the face of difficult landscapes and challenges.

Story:

Three lions lived in an African jungle. One day, the monkey – the representative chosen by the animals – called a meeting of all the inhabitants to pose an important question:

"Dear friends," he said. We all know that the lion is the king of the jungle, but in our territory we have three very strong, young lions. As a jungle cannot have three kings, which one should we obey?"

The animals reached a decision and told the three lions:

"We've decided that the three of you are going to climb to the top of the Difficult Mountain. The lion that arrives there first will be recognized as king."

The first lion tried to climb the mountain, but couldn't. The second began with a lot of enthusiasm, but he too was soon defeated. The third lion couldn't manage it, either. How would the animals choose their king? Then a wise eagle asked permission to speak in the assembly:

"I know who our king should be!" he declared.

"How do you know?" the animals asked.

"It's easy," said the eagle. "I was flying nearby when each of them turned back. And I heard what they were saying."

The first lion said, 'Mountain, you've defeated me!' The second one said, 'Mountain, you're stupid, you'll pay for this!'

The third one said, 'Mountain, I didn't manage it, for now! But you've already reached your full size, whereas I'm still growing!'

✺ Reflections on the situation

- Which lion do you think the jungle animals crowned, and why?

- What were the differences in attitude among the three lions?

- Which attitude do you think is the most passive?

- Which do you think is the most aggressive?

- Which one keeps open the possibility of achieving the climb?

- What kind of attitude do you usually have when you face a major difficulty?

- What conclusions do you draw from this tale?

✺ Conclusions for further work

Life often tests us, and we cannot always achieve every objective we set for ourselves, but if it is important to us, it is up to us to keep trying.

Not achieving something is not equivalent to failure; it just means not achieving it for now.

There are three kinds of attitude, or ways of behaving, that we can put into practice when facing a problem: do nothing (a passive attitude), get angry and fight with everyone (an aggressive attitude), or fight to solve the problem (an assertive attitude).

The posture of the third lion is assertive and is the attitude of someone who fights actively to achieve the things that matter to him/her, but respectfully and without attacking others.

How to change in order to continue being yourself

☀ Objective:

To understand that at difficult moments we sometimes have to change if we don't want to lose ourselves. To discuss the question of loss and trust.

Story:

After crossing mountains and plains, a river reached the desert sand and tried to cross it. Then it saw that its waters would disappear into the sand as soon as it entered the desert. And though it was convinced that its destiny was to cross the sand, it could find no way to do so. Suddenly it heard a voice that said:

"If the wind crosses the desert, the river can too."

"But the wind can fly, and I'll be absorbed by the sand," said the river.

"If you rush forward violently, as you have done until now, you won't achieve it; you will disappear or turn into a swamp. You must let the wind carry you to your destiny," said the voice.

"But how can I manage what you're telling me to do?" asked the river.

"You must let the wind absorb you," the voice said.

The river wasn't pleased with this idea. It had never been absorbed before and it didn't want to lose its individuality.

"How can I know for sure that, once I lose my shape, I'll be able to recover it?" the river asked.

"The wind fulfils its function. It raises the water, transports it to its destination, and drops it as rain. This is how the water returns to the river," said the voice.

"But can't I go on being the same river as I am now?" asked the river.

"No," the voice replied. "Your essence will be carried away and form a new river."

The river wasn't too sure, but it didn't want to turn into a swamp or disappear. So, in an act of trust, it raised its vapor into the welcoming arms of the wind, who gently carried it up and away, and then dropped it on top of the mountain as rain. This is how the water became a river again.

☀ Reflections on the story

- Why do you think the river finds it difficult to trust the wind? What is it afraid of?

- What would happen to the river if it didn't change from its liquid state to a gaseous one?

- Is the water still water when it is vapor? And when it is solid? What do you think is the essence of water?

- What is it that does not change in people, even when they get old or many unexpected things happen to them?

☀ Conclusions for further work

During our lives we will have to cross more than one "desert." Emotional deserts are critical situations in which we feel alone and scared of what might happen.

To cross a desert, it is important to travel light. If we just keep what's essential, it will be easier to cross.

Trust in ourselves and in others enables us to keep going when the path becomes difficult. Somehow we feel that we are going to know how to find the solution to each obstacle that might arise.

WHAT WOULD YOU BE IF YOU WERE . . . ?

⊛ Objective:

To identify qualities and characteristics in oneself. To do an exercise in self-knowledge and discover a different way of presenting oneself to a group.

Activity:

The group sits in a circle and the leader starts a sentence that each person repeats, completing the sentence to describe him/herself. Example: "If I were an animal, I would be a deer."

If I were . . . I would be . . .

The following items of comparison are suggested: if I were a planet, a landscape, a plant, an animal, a season of the year, a month, a tune, a color, etc.

Each participant writes down his/her choice and then thinks of three characteristics of that item and jots them down. For example:

If I were a season of the year, I'd be summer, because I am warm, deliberate, and sociable.

⊛ Reflections on the activity

- Can you make a list of all the qualities you discovered in yourself while doing this exercise?

- Was it difficult to extract your characteristics from what you had chosen?

- What conclusions do you draw about yourself? And about the rest of the group?

- What did it feel like doing this task? Do you think your group is diverse? Why?

⊛ Conclusions for further work

Everything that surrounds us reflects us in a way similar to a mirror. It is very important to know how to look.

The same exercise done at different times would have different results, since our emotions are not static and may vary from moment to moment. For example, you may feel happy now, even if you felt sad earlier in the day. However, our personality traits are more stable and evolve more slowly. If you are a sociable person, you will continue to be so, regardless of how you are feeling at any particular time.

Shipwreck on a Desert Island

Objective:

To distinguish what is basic from what is superfluous to survival. To learn to negotiate and compromise. To work on the values that underlie our decisions.

Activity:

You have been shipwrecked and are on an uninhabited island with no link to the rest of the world. Then a wizard appears and gives you the chance to choose ten survival resources from those that appear on the list that follows.

Each participant first draws up his/her own list. Then each group (of four or five people) has forty-five minutes to hand in its final list, agreed on unanimously.

Additional information to consider in making a good choice:

1. The island measures twelve miles from one side to the other. Of its surface area,

   −a quarter is a lake teeming with fish

   −a quarter is cultivatable land

   −a quarter is a wild forest

   −a quarter is uncultivated land

2. The place is agreeable, with a summery climate and a constant temperature of 86°F during the day and 68°F at night. It rains only thirty days a year.

- A full fishing kit
- Two spades and two pick-axes
- A cow and a bull
- Three tennis racquets and twenty balls
- Two guitars
- Twenty swimsuits
- A video-console with five kinds of games
- One hundred boxes of assorted preserved foods
- One hundred books of classic literature
- One hundred bottles of alcoholic drink
- A new Jeep
- A boat without oars
- Ten metal bars
- One hundred boxes of matches
- A large amount of antibiotics
- A horse
- One hundred packs of cigarettes
- A Siamese cat
- Toiletries and beauty supplies
- Various kinds of seeds
- A personal computer
- Twenty-five photographs of well-known people
- Five thousand sheets of writing paper
- A rifle and one hundred bullets
- Thirty tubes of oil paint
- An MP3 player
- 4 thousand liters of petrol
- A GPS
- Two three-person camping tents
- Three big beds

Reflections on the activity

- How would you feel if you thought you would pass the rest of your life on the desert island?

- What part of this activity was most difficult for you?

- How many of the objects chosen in your first list were included in the final list? What emotions did you feel during the group discussion? Did you feel satisfied with the final result?

Conclusions for further work

In real life we only really "have" what we cannot lose in a shipwreck, "ourselves." The rest comes and goes.

At difficult moments, it is important to make decisions and know what is a priority and what we can do without.

THE
KOI
FISH

- Do you think the size of a fish can depend **on the size of the fish tank in which it lives?**
- **What conditions in the natural and human environment DO YOU THINK AFFECT YOUR GROWTH?**
- **What can you do TO IMPROVE THE PLACE WHERE YOU LIVE?**

Did you know that the favorite fish of many collectors is the Japanese carp called the koi fish? The fish's most fascinating feature is that its size depends on the size of the place where it lives: if it lives in a small fishbowl, it grows only a few inches; if we move it to a small pond, it can reach a foot long; and if it lives in an even bigger pond, it can reach a foot and a half. The biggest koi, in a big lake, are three feet in length!

Did you know that dolphins in freedom live to an average age of about forty, whereas in captivity they only live about eight years, even though they receive regular veterinary care and monitoring?

Had you noticed that, even in the best zoos, the animals get ill because they are fenced in and are a long way from their natural environment? This happens to both captured animals and those born in captivity. Many of them behave strangely, repeat movements obsessively, lose their appetite, are sad, or show aggressive behavior.

✳ Let's think...

- What might happen when an animal or plant does not have enough space? Why do dolphins have a shorter lifespan in captivity? How do you think they feel?

- Can you compare this with what happens to people who have limited freedom or resources (food, water, education, or affection)?

- Do you think we look after the environment properly?

- How does our behavior affect animals and plants?

Animals, plants, and people

need a proper space to fully develop.

The place where we live conditions our physical and emotional growth, though we can change and improve the areas we live in (habitat): our home, school, neighborhood, city, or country.

We do not have to live in a fish bowl. If you were a fish, where would you prefer to swim, in a fish bowl or a lake?

☀ Let's think...

- How can you know whether your space meets the conditions needed to grow properly?

- Have you ever felt overwhelmed? Did someone invade your space? What happened?

- What did you do to solve it?

- How do you feel when someone says no to something you want?

- Do you think there is a difference between a limit and a prison? Can you think of an example?

- Can you find an example of a situation in which you feel especially happy and free?

WHAT EMOTIONS DO YOU FEEL WHEN SOMEONE INVADES YOUR SPACE? HOW DO YOU BEHAVE?

IN WHAT DIFFERENT WAYS DO YOU MARK
YOUR PERSONAL PROPERTY
AND TERRITORY?

LEAVING THE MAZE

⚙ Objective:

To learn to trust in oneself and others. To work on attention and listening. To realize how important our visual sense is for orienting ourselves.

Activity:

A maze is assembled in the room (tables and chairs can be used to mark boundaries). The maze has to have one way in and one way out. There should also be areas with no exit and obstacles on the paths.

Once the maze has been set up, the participants are asked to move through it with a blindfold, orienting themselves only on the basis of the instructions given by their partner, who guides them without touching them.

With a few minutes between them, the pairs enter the maze. When they reach the end, they sit in silence and watch the other participants.

Then the maze is restructured. Its shape is changed and the pairs exchange roles.

⚙ Reflections on the activity

- How did you feel during the exercise? Did you trust your partner? Were you afraid? What were you afraid of?

- Did you bump into anything? If you did, what did you think? What did you feel like? Did you get annoyed with your partner?

- Have you ever felt anything like what you felt when you went through the maze blindfolded?

- What do you think it would have been like if, instead of having a guide, you had to find the exit yourself?

- If your partner had guided you by the shoulder, would you have felt better? Why?

- Would you have felt more confident if you had been able to memorize a map of the maze before the exercise?

⚙ Conclusions for further work

Sometimes life seems like a maze: there are paths that lead nowhere and others that take the long way round. Sometimes we get lost and we think we won't find the exit. Then it is normal to feel insecure and fearful.

If we listen to those who know the route better than we do, we will be better oriented.

Our parents, friends, teachers, and other people can be our guides at particular moments. A good guide is essential. There are guides who are even more lost than we are, which means that the instructions they give us may make our journey more difficult. So as not to go blindly through life, it is important to be familiar with the spaces in which we move, to trust ourselves, and surround ourselves with good "guides."

ANIMALS IN SEARCH OF A HOME

⊛ Objective:

To realize that every living being needs particular conditions to grow and develop in a balanced way. If an animal's habitat is inadequate, it becomes ill and dies.

Activity:

Manifesto of animal territoriality

This place is mine, I come from here, say the albatross, the monkey, the green moon fish, the great owl, the wolf, the bulldog, the prairie dog, the ringed plover, the blowfish, the Rocky Mountain salmon
. . . I come from here, from this place on Earth and I share the identity of this place. And this is something no one can take away from me, despite all the sufferings I may undergo, where I may go, or where I die. I will always belong solely to this place.

The manifesto of animal territoriality is read aloud and discussed. Then groups of two to four people are formed and a series of drawings or photos of animals are distributed (albatross, moon fish, lion, elephant, lynx, koala bear). Each team has to research on the Internet the preferred territory of each animal and the territory's basic conditions (space, humidity, temperature, etc.), and place the animal in its appropriate habitat on the map. You will need a large world map on the wall where you can place the figure of each animal.

⊛ Reflections on the activity

- Why does each animal need to live in a particular habitat?

- In what part of the planet do you live?

- Can you think of three basic conditions your habitat should have?

- What three emotions would you like to see grow in your territory?

⊛ Conclusions for further work

We have a house outside us, in which we live: the ecosystem Earth. It contains our country, city or village, school, and family. All of them make up the various habitats we are part of.

At the same time, we have an inner house, where our memories, desires, thoughts, and emotions reside. It is where we go when outside circumstances are difficult or change too quickly.

Disconnected from ourselves, we feel lost and sad. It is important to understand our inner ecosystem, to know what makes us feel good and bad, and work to take care of this territory, since our personal equilibrium depends on it.

MARKING OUT OUR TERRITORY

⚙ Objective:

Human beings also have ways of placing boundaries around our territory and preventing it from being invaded.

Activity:

Think of the territorial signs we use to tell other people that:

- A chair is occupied.
- A house is ours.
- A uniform belongs to us.
- A whole section of table is for us.
- We're different from the rest.
- Someone is religious.
- We don't want someone to come into our room.
- It is forbidden to continue along a road.
- We belong to a particular family.
- We are part of a particular country or nation.
- It is dangerous to enter a particular place.
- Someone is married.
- Access to a website is restricted.

⚙ Reflections on the activity

- Did you know that lions meet in herds, or prides, to defend their territory from other animals? And that wolves mark their territories through smell signals, using their urine and feces? And that cats define it by scratching objects with their claws? And that some birds mark territory through sounds or the colors of their feathers?

- Why do you think protection and defending a territory is so important in the animal kingdom?

- What do we feel and how do we behave when we feel invaded?

⚙ Conclusions for further work

We are territorial beings. Like animals, each of us needs space to feel relaxed.

Some people are comfortable in small, closed spaces, whereas others need large, open spaces. This is neither good nor bad, but another signal that we are different.

If we want to live in harmony, we must learn to understand and respect others' territorial marks and signals.

Handkerchiefs or personal objects, flags, notices, signs, barriers, fences, borders, clothes and accessories, locks, surnames, rings, crosses, and access codes are all ways of marking a territory. They indicate whether you belong and can enter a space, or whether you have to stay outside.

When people do not respect these rules, they invade others' territory and cause conflict.

A SOLIDARITY TEA PARTY

🤝 Objective:

To experience in our own skin how the unjust distribution of resources available in our ecosystem affects us.

Activity:

The children are invited to a party, and each child brings a food item from home. As everyone gathers, they are given an envelope containing a red card or a green card.

The red card reads: "You are part of the 80% of the world's population that have access to only 20% of the planet's resources."

The green card reads: "You are part of the 20% of the world's population that consume 80% of the planet's resources."

If there are twenty people in the group, sixteen red cards and four green cards are given out.

Then two tables are prepared: a small table with sixteen chairs and 20% of the food; and a big table, with four chairs and 80% of the food.

The children are told they can begin eating, and their reactions and behavior are observed. It would be interesting to record the event on video.

Once they have experienced how they feel in their assigned roles, the initial layout is restored and all the food is shared equally.

🤔 Reflections on the activity

- Which part of the population did you belong to?

- How did you feel when you found out (angry, content, ashamed, sad, indignant, envious, irritated, proud . . .)?

- What did you say or do during the group dynamic? Did anyone try to change the situation?

- Do you think it's fair that 20% of the people can use 80% of the planet's resources? Why do you think this happens? Can you do anything to make the world a fairer place, with more solidarity?

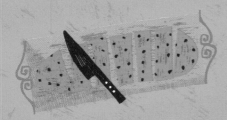

⚙️ Conclusions for further work

Our planet possesses sufficient resources for everyone to be able to live on it. Air, water, food, the land, and energy sources are resources, as are access to education, health, and jobs.

When some people monopolize resources, others are left without them. For example, while some people are overfed, others go hungry; while some accumulate wealth, others suffer poverty. The resources are there, but they are badly distributed.

When a plant, animal, or human being is left without the space and resources it needs, it stops growing, falls ill, and dies.

Unjust situations cause rage, anger, resentment, frustration, and hatred, whereas fair situations create gratitude, friendship, joy, calm, and emotional well-being.

LOSING TO WIN

✿ Objective:

To be aware that we have to accept living temporarily in the discomfort of what we do not know. In uncertain territories, we feel weak and unprotected, but these are great opportunities for growth.

Situation:

The lobster is related to the river crab.

Although it looks slow, it can swim and move rapidly, thanks to the sharp contraction of its abdomen.

To be able to grow, it has to get rid of the shell that protects it, which makes it vulnerable to predator attack.

The animal eats its empty shell, which replaces the calcium its body needs.

⚙ Reflections on the situation

- Why do you think lobsters have to get rid of their shells to grow?

- What do you think might happen to the lobster when it is no longer protected by the shell?

- What would happen if the lobster refused to get rid of its shell for a time?

- What is a predator? What predatory animals can you think of?

- Do human beings use shells to protect our territory and intimacy?

⚙ Conclusions for further work

To evolve and grow, we have to get rid of what compresses and restricts us. Our shell may consist of various things: "I can't" thoughts, old ideas, inherited rules, guilt, resentments, fears, or thoughts of "it's not important."

Human predators are aggressive or insecure people who try to feel powerful by mistreating weaker and more vulnerable people.

If we were getting rid of a shell that is no longer useful to us, we will feel defenseless and alone until we construct better, suitable protection. Then we will feel freer and happier.

TOO MANY CAGES, TOO MANY WALLS

⊛ Objective:

To become aware of how the loss of freedom affects us. To work on the capacity for empathy and look for emotionally ecological ways of behaving.

Activity:

Participants are divided into three groups:

One group will build small cages with cardboard boxes. The figures of ten animals, made of paper, cardboard, or play dough, will be placed inside, prisoners in cages, whether at home or at the zoo.

The children are asked to write on a piece of paper how they think they would feel if they were caged like the animals.

Another group will build a wall (3 feet long and 18 inches high) out of cardboard boxes or newspaper.

This group will investigate how many walls are currently raised between countries and will list the countries on their wall.

They will also write down how they would feel if their country was walled in.

The third group will cut out an 18-inch-diameter heart, paint it red, and place it in a fenced-in place. They are asked to think about all the things we don't let out of ourselves (thoughts we don't dare express, emotions we hold in, things we do not dare to do, and fears that do not let us move forward). They will write these things on pieces of paper and stick them on the heart.

⊙ Reflections on the activity

- Why do you think human beings build cages, prisons, and walls?

- What emotions did you feel while doing this exercise? How do you think you'd feel toward the person who stops you from leaving the cage or crossing the wall?

- Can you investigate the famous Berlin Wall? When and why was it built? How did it affect and separate families? How and when was it demolished?

- Can you imagine a world without barriers? What two actions could you take to create this world, little by little?

⊛ Conclusions for further work

Birds were born to fly through the air, dolphins to swim in the sea, and lions to run across plains. Animals need to be with their own species in a natural environment; they get sick when we imprison them.

Cages and prisons are human inventions. Locking someone up is cruel. Nature puts no walls between countries: walls result from fear and ignorance. They arise because of fear of things that are different, anguish in the face of the unknown, or panic at losing what we think is ours.

Sometimes we close ourselves off inside and don't tell others what we think, feel, or want. This is also a form of prison that may damage us. The cages have to be opened and the walls knocked down.

MAPS AND DRAGONS

- **WHAT PART OF THE PLANET EARTH HAVE YOU GOTTEN TO KNOW DIRECTLY?**
- **WHAT PARTS OF YOURSELF DO YOU KNOW?**
- **DO YOU THINK AN OLD MAP IS ANY USE FOR GUIDING US THROUGH TODAY'S WORLD?**

Centuries ago, the cartographers had the custom of drawing a dragon at the point where the known world ended. The dragon symbol told explorers they were entering unknown territory, and to proceed at their own risk. Unfortunately, some people thought the dragon on the map really existed and were frightened of continuing with their exploration. Others were bolder and saw new opportunities in this symbol. They marched forward and found no dragons, but rather new lands full of treasures and wealth.

Since the beginning of history, humans have been explorers. Slowly but unceasingly, we have conquered remote areas of the Earth. In 1911, the Norwegian Roald Amundsen reached the most recent region of the globe to be explored, Antarctica.

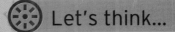

Let's think...

- Do you know the names of any explorers?
- What difficulties do you think they had to overcome before managing to conquer new lands?
- What fears did they have to face?
- Why do you think they devoted their lives to venturing into unknown lands?

Map

Inside ourselves, there is also a whole world to explore. From birth we start to follow its paths, and when we learn something, we write it down on a kind of inner map. If it went well, we put up a sign saying "free entry," and if it went badly, we place signs to warn us of danger.

Often, when someone harms us, we put up walls to defend ourselves and, though these walls do protect us, they may also leave us alone and isolated. In our lives, dragons are the fears that paralyze or stop us, and prevent us from broadening our territory and discovering new things. We can face up to our dragons, take a risk, and trust in finding the best response, or we can stay in secure, known territory. Only we can decide.

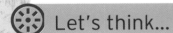 Let's think...

- How do you feel when you stop doing things you want to do because you haven't faced up to your fears?

- Have you looked directly at any dragon-fear?

- Are there many dragons in your life? What are they called?

- What do you think would happen if you dared to enter dragon territory?

- How do you think you'd feel if you managed to make them disappear?

HOW CAN YOU FEED CONFIDENCE AND MAKE IT GROW?

TOO MUCH ROUTINE

⚙ Objective:

To realize we have more space than we think. Sometimes we don't see this because, if we just repeat routines, we fail to see everything else.

Situation:

The other day we went to a friend's house. We found him engaged in "the ceremony of cleaning his fish bowl."

He told us it was important to change the water and clean it thoroughly quite often. He went on talking while he carefully continued his cleaning ritual.

First, he filled a bathtub with water at the right temperature.

Then he caught the fish in a net and placed them carefully in the bath water. Our friend emptied the water from the fish bowl, cleaned it, and filled it again. When we went to put the fish back in their bowl, how surprised we were to see that, although the bathtub was big, the fish maintained a circular swimming route that was quite small, similar to the size of their fish bowl!

⚙ Reflections on the situation

- Why do you think the fish continued swimming in a small circle?

- What do you think would happen if the fish took a slightly bigger risk?

- Do you like repetition? What things do you do every day the same way? What benefits are there in doing it like this? How do you feel?

- What can we lose if we don't try to do things differently?

- When you do something new, do you feel afraid? Of what? And when the new thing turns out well, how do you feel?

⚙ Conclusions for further work

Some routines serve to save us energy, and it is a good idea to maintain them. For example, we often behave automatically when we've experienced something and know it works.

Other routines and automatic behaviors end up closing off paths, as they make us stay in secure, familiar places and not try to improve our situation.

Accepting something as known or normal may halt our learning. We shouldn't forget that living means gaining inner and external territories.

A child is an explorer by nature. It is important to maintain this spirit of adventure and curiosity all our lives.

GIVE YOUR DRAGONS A NAME

⊛ Objective:

To name our main fears. When they have a name, they are no longer so terrible, and we can work with them. The fact of seeing that we all have fears and that some of them are common will help us face them.

Activity:

Each child receives a blank piece of paper and is asked to draw a map of the main areas of his/her life: family, school, friends, and activities. The size of each area should correspond to the importance the child gives it.

The children are also given a piece of paper with small drawings of dragons that can be cut out.

The exercise involves thinking about each area they've drawn on the map and detecting where they think there might be some kind of fear or obstacle.

For example, the Fear Dragon might appear each time there's a swimming class coming up, or the Embarrassment Dragon might appear when you have to explain something before the whole class.

Once these fears are identified, each child cuts out a dragon and sticks it in the appropriate area.

The activity is shared and a common list of all the dragons detected is drawn up.

⊛ Reflections on the activity

- In what areas of your life are there dragons? Are they big or small? What are they called?

- Do you remember any occasion when something that frightened you ended up being something you really like doing?

- Can you make a list of strategies you use to make your fears vanish?

⊛ Conclusions for further work

From birth we construct a mental map of ourselves, others, and the world. In it we place signs to guide us, indicators of the obstacles we will have to overcome if we take that route again, and we note the best paths, the result of positive or negative experiences.

In the ancient world, the dragon symbol meant: "Adventurer, if you follow this path, we cannot tell you what you are going to find because it is an unexplored area." But many people have turned it into "Access forbidden" or a symbol of danger. When we go on despite our fears, we realize that often these dragons disappear and we activate resources we didn't know we had. Identifying a dragon is equivalent to locating a space for personal growth.

TIED TO A STAKE

⚙ Objective:

To became aware that saying "I can't" is a stake that makes us prisoners. To realize that, as we grow, we learn new things that can be used to solve old problems and "free us from the stakes."

Situation:

One day a child saw a circus elephant tied by a rope to a small stake knocked into the ground. He was surprised that such a big animal could not get free and, what's more, made no effort to do so. He decided to ask the keeper, who answered: "It's very simple. When it was small, we tied it to this stake. Then it tried to get free, but it wasn't yet strong enough to do so. After a time it gave up trying. Now the elephant is unaware of its strength, as it has never tested it out. Because it thinks freedom is impossible, it's never even tried to get free. With its present strength, it would have no difficulty, but it lives tied to something that only exists in its imagination."

⚙ Reflections on the situation

- How do you think the little elephant felt when it was tied to the stake for the first time? Why did it stop trying to get free? Do you think the bigger elephant knows how strong it is? Why?

- Have you ever been certain that you couldn't get free of something or that you wouldn't achieve something you wanted? How did you feel?

- Have you ever used the word "impossible" or the phrase "I can't"? Can you remember the situation and what happened in the end?

⚙ Conclusions for further work

The thought "I can't" reduces our territory and restricts us. It is important to eliminate it from our vocabulary. We can always replace it with: "At present I can't, but I'm going to struggle and learn new things so I can in the future."

When we do not fight for our freedom, we feel sad, impotent, dispirited, weak. However, if we do struggle for it, we feel full of energy, strength, and courage.

When we achieve something that was hard for us, we feel happy, and this increases our conquered territory. Undoubtedly, the greatest failure is not failing to achieve something we've tried to do, but to never have tried.

EXPLORING MYSELF

⊛ Objective:

To be aware of all the wealth we have inside us, and in the process learn to value ourselves more highly.

Activity:

Participants are asked to draw a large human silhouette on a piece of paper. They will draw a brain on the head; eyes, ears, nose, and mouth on the face; a heart on the chest, and so on.

Then each person is given a piece of paper with a series of questions. He or she writes down the answers and connects them with an arrow to the appropriate organ:

- **What are the five best ideas you have had in your life?**
- **What are the five most beautiful things you have seen?**
- **What five words do you most like people to say to you?**
- **What five things do you most like to taste?**
- **What five aromas do you most like to smell?**
- **What five things do you most like to do and touch?**
- **What five emotions do you most like to feel?**
- **What five people do you carry in your heart?**

The participants share their discoveries with the group.

⊛ Reflections on the activity

- How did you feel doing this exercise?
- What part of your body was easiest for you to work on? Which part was the most complicated? Why?
- Were your answers similar to those of the group?
- Do you put into practice what you like? If you like people to say a word to you, do you say it to others? If you have a good idea, do you put it into practice?

⊛ Conclusions for further work

Our bodies, minds, and "hearts" are full of treasures ready to be discovered. We may have good ideas, excellent feelings, and many abilities, but if we don't convert them into concrete actions, they are no use. It would be like having treasure buried on our territory: what use would it be?

Understanding our own map and its treasures allows us to discover the treasures of others, improve our lives, and cultivate happiness.

CUTTING THE BRANCH

⊛ Objective:

To become aware that sometimes it takes an extreme event to get people to leave their comfort zone.

Story:

A king was given two small falcons and handed them to the falconry master for training. After several months, the master told the king that one of the falcons was perfectly trained, but that the other had not moved from the branch where they had put it on the very first day. He didn't know what was wrong. The king called healers and specialists from every corner of his kingdom to examine the falcon, but no one could get it to fly. The next day, from his window, the king saw that the bird was still immobile. Then he decided to issue a proclamation, offering a reward to the person who got the falcon to fly.

The following morning, he saw the falcon flying smoothly round the gardens.

The king said to the court:

"Bring me the person who produced this miracle."

Soon they brought in a peasant. The king asked him:

"Did you make the falcon fly? How did you manage it? Are you a wizard?"

The peasant humbly replied:

"It was easy, your majesty. I just cut off the branch where it was resting. The falcon realized it had wings and launched itself into flight."

⊛ Reflections on the story

- Why do you think one falcon flew and the other didn't? Have you ever been in a situation where you felt paralyzed and you didn't do what you really wanted to do?

- Can you think of a situation you found difficult? Like what happened to the falcon in the story, did someone "cut off your branch" so that you could begin to fly?

- The falcon realized it had wings and then flew. If wings are its resources, what do you think yours were on this occasion? What would give you confidence to become capable of doing something new or daring?

- Can you think of other ways to get the falcon to react?

- Could you invent another ending to the story?

⊛ Conclusions for further work

Fear may paralyze us, but so can comfort. You have to abandon routines to conquer new things. If we remain passive, without doing what our nature suggests, we are going to miss a lot of opportunities.

If we are born with wings, they are for flying. If we are born with intelligence, it is to improve our life and the lives of others. If we are born with emotions and feelings, it is to be more human with each other and know how to protect ourselves.

To grow is to gain confidence and conquer new territories.

WHAT'S NEW IN YOUR LIFE?

Objective:

To become aware of the most important changes you have experienced since birth, the changes you are experiencing now, and those you think will come soon.

Activity:

Participants make a chronological list of the most important changes in their lives since birth.

During the week, the children research these changes by asking parents, family members, and friends about them. Examples are moving to a new house or school, a change in babysitter or guardian, making a new friend or losing a friend, divorce or separation of parents, illness, and so on. Once all the information is in, the child makes a chronological list of each "change event" and writes in a different color what he/she learned from living through it.

The second stage of the exercise involves writing down the main changes they think await them in the next five years: change of school, physical changes, new relationships, holidays, journeys, and so on.

Beside each future change, children write in a different color the emotion they feel when they think about the change: curiosity, happiness, bewilderment, insecurity, sorrow, etc.

If they detect any dragon-fear, they must try to name it: for example, the dragon-fear is that I won't manage it.

Reflections on the activity

- How did you feel about researching all the changes in your life? What did you learn?

- What emotions do you feel most often when you think of the changes that await you?

- What do you think would have happened in your life if you hadn't adapted to changes that occurred?

- What could help you feel more confident before future changes?

- Can you make a list of all the good things you hope to achieve in your life?

Conclusions for further work

Nothing is static. Everything changes – the seasons, the air temperature, our bodies, our way of thinking, our feelings, and even the ideas we have about ourselves. Change creates uncertainty. This is why we feel frustrated when changes occur.

We search for security because we lack confidence. Security involves avoiding the surprise effect that can throw us off balance. Thus, we become comfortable and resigned to routine. However, confidence lets us live through change without feeling disturbed. It is not the absence of fear, but the ability to do what has to be done despite our feelings.

CREATE PROTECTED SPACES

- WHAT IS A **PROTECTED SPACE?**
- HOW MANY SPECIES DO YOU THINK ARE **CURRENTLY IN DANGER OF EXTINCTION?**
- DID YOU KNOW THAT PARTICULAR VALUES AND FEELINGS **ALSO NEED TO BE CONSERVED?**

53

There are unique species

that can only grow in pollution-free places. We are responsible for conserving their habitats and the conditions that make their lives possible.

Lowlands and tropical forests are the habitats where the greatest number of threatened mammals and birds live. Sweet-water habitats are also highly vulnerable; they are home to many species of fish, reptiles, amphibians, and invertebrates.

Let's think...

- Did you know that 16,300 species of animals and plants are in danger of extinction, and that 1,200 of these are found in the Iberian peninsula?

- Did you know that the Iberian lynx, an Asian antelope, and the wild camel are the species at the greatest risk of extinction?

- Life is disappearing rapidly from the Earth and will continue to do so unless urgent action is taken. This is why conservation organizations are trying to stop species extinction. They have taken various actions, one of which is to create nature reserves where ecological balance can be maintained.

Inside us we also need to create protected spaces where fragile feelings and values, which need special care, can grow. These are valuable environments that cannot be replaced, special places that let us appreciate the beauty and wonder of life in its purest state.

What emotions do you think we should conserve in order to be happier?

Here are some ideas:

- **Gratitude,** for everything good that life gives us.

- **Friendship,** which accompanies us and helps us grow along with others.

- **Love,** which is the most creative energy and the best path to balance and happiness.

- **Trust,** the key to all personal relationships.

- **Compassion,** which means solidarity and sharing others' suffering, along with actions to improve our world.

- **Hope,** a powerful light that lets us work for a better future.

- **Happiness,** which arises from internal equilibrium.

- **Generosity,** which is an emotionally sustainable energy.

- **Tenderness,** which brings out the best in us, respects the rhythms of others, and gives warmth to our world.

WHAT CAN YOU DO SO THAT **LOVE, TENDERNESS, AND COMPASSION** DO NOT DISAPPEAR FROM THIS WORLD?

I AM A WORLD HERITAGE SITE

✿ Objective:

To realize that we are unique species and that no one like us will ever exist again. To learn to protect our diversity and create proper conditions for it to thrive.

Activity:

Imagine that you are going to apply to UNESCO for recognition as an Emotional Heritage Site.

You have to write a letter giving at least ten reasons why you should be considered unique, special, and valuable.

You can finish the letter with the phrase " . . . and for all the above, I request that [your name] be declared a World Heritage Site," followed by the date and your signature. Once finished, each participant reads their letter aloud and hangs it on a mural.

Background music should accompany the activity. The participants then search for a letter with at least three characteristics similar to their own. The letters are put together and surrounded by a circle that is given a name, "[. . .] habitat."

For fifteen minutes, each affinity group talks about what the world (family, school, friends) would lose if they weren't there.

✿ Reflections on the activity

- What is UNESCO? What's the purpose of declaring something a World Heritage Site?

- Can you make a list of everything you like about the people who surround you? Do you think these characteristics should be protected?

- Do you think people are born with these characteristics or that they cultivate them over time?

- What is your most important feeling to protect to be happy?

- What can do the most damage to this unique species that you are? What can you do to improve your habitat?

✿ Conclusions for further work

Life is a great gift, and in it are people with whom we share affinities and characteristics. Similar to what happens in the animal and plant worlds, different species can share spaces in equilibrium.

One of the laws of emotional ecology is the Law of Diversity: natural life depends on its diversity and wealth. There never has been, nor ever will be, a person identical to us. This makes us unique, valuable, and worthy of respect. We must not agree to being mistreated or attacked.

We have great emotional wealth. Each emotion has its color, nature, and function.

Emotional diversity protects us. There are emotional species that make the world better, and we must create habitats suited to their growth.

MY RED LIST

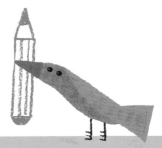

Objective:

To realize that there are characteristics, values, qualities, and emotions that can be lost if the spaces they need are not protected.

Activity:

For a week, each child researches species in danger of extinction, looking for information and pictures of the three species that have had most impact on the child.

The children are also asked to think of three pleasant emotions that make them feel good. They should name the emotions, look for information about them, and think of a color or image that represents them.

Groups of five children each get together to share what they've come up with. Each group will make two murals; one on the natural species they've researched, and the other on the emotions that make them feel good and need to be protected. The names of the species and emotions are written next to the images, along with the reasons they should be conserved and cared for.

When the two murals are finished, each group explains to the others which natural species and which emotions they are going to protect and why.

Reflections on the activity

- What human behavior damages biodiversity and accelerates species extinction?

- Which five emotional species are most highly ranked by all the participants?

- Can you imagine what would happen if we lost them? What would the world be like?

- Concretely, what can we do to look after these species?

Conclusions for further work

To look after something, first we have to be aware that it is valuable.

Each species requires specific habitat conditions. If it has them, it grows and develops; if not, it gets sick and dies.

Extinction is an evolutionary process that is part of natural selection. The problem is that human beings are speeding up this process, due to destructive behaviors that are often unconscious.

Certain emotions, feelings, and values are found on the Red List of species in danger. It is important to be aware of this, so that we can take small actions every day to conserve them and foster their growth.

THE "SNAKES AND LADDERS" OF EMOTIONAL DIVERSITY

✲ Objective:

To familiarize yourself with different emotions. To become aware of the factors that stimulate them and the conditions that make them disappear. To improve emotional vocabulary.

Activity:

Groups of five create a game board using the classic international game Snakes and Ladders as a model, but decorating it with motifs from the world of emotions.

The aim is to reach the treasure of happiness at the center, which contains all the valuable affections we must protect. Participants place obstacles on the road such as the fire of anger, the precipice of violence, the prison of prejudice, derailment due to hurry, the pit of sadness, the desert of loneliness, the toll of discouragement, the burden of guilt. To get out of the traps, the player has to answer questions from a previously prepared envelope marked with the number of the trap-square they've landed on, or do an activity.

Accelerators can also be placed on the route, such as a kite, which lets players jump forward ten squares; an emotional pot of jam, which provides an energy boost; an emotional GPS – whatever the group imagines.

Before starting, it will be helpful for each team to look for information on the most basic emotions: fear, sadness, happiness, disgust, anger, surprise.

They must also create a manual explaining the rules. The teams exchange boards and play the game.

✪ Reflections on the activity

- At what point on the Snakes and Ladders board are you now? How did you feel when you made the board as a team? What was the hardest part?

- What images or colors represented the different emotions?

- What did you have to do to overcome the main obstacles?

- What emotion gives you energy? What emotions cause you suffering?

- What's the most important thing you've learned in this game about emotions?

✪ Conclusions for further work

We cannot get rid of unpleasant emotions, as we do not choose them - we feel them. The most important thing is to learn what we can do to give them proper, responsible expression. For example, we can learn that we have to get rid of the guilt and prejudices that immobilize us, and transform them into responsibility and generosity. That with the energy of anger we can leap over obstacles and overcome injustice. That fear can protect us if we don't let it dominate us.

We can learn from each other if we want to, if we listen and ask, since each of us experiences emotions differently.

A GARDEN IN THE CLASSROOM

✺ Objective:

To become aware of how diverse we are and understand that when we improve ourselves, we enrich the entire ecosystem to which we belong, whether it is family, school, our community, or the world.

Activity:

"Plant" a garden where each flower represents the best quality that each person contributes to the group. We will need card stock, crayons, watercolors, felt-tip pens, and all kinds of recycled materials used to adorn each flower.

Each child is given a card on which to draw, cut out, and decorate a flower. On the back, the children write the qualities they most value in themselves.

Then a "care sheet" is passed out to each child, to be filled in with observations on the type of habitat it prefers, the conditions that help it grow, and what precautions should be taken to prevent it from becoming sick. The children also write down other species it is compatible or incompatible with and what kind of compost or emotional nutrition it needs.

The participants introduce their flower, explaining the care it needs, and then place it on a prepared mural titled "The Classroom Garden."

⊡ Reflections on the activity

- Was it difficult to decide the colors and shape of your flower? Is it big or small? Why?

- Do you like the "flower" you are?

- What other flowers do you live with in your family and at school?

- What emotional climate harms your flower? What conditions does it need to live well? How is it like other flowers? How is it different?

- What is the best part of the classroom garden? What resources do you share? What happens if one person monopolizes the best resources and doesn't leave enough for the rest?

✺ Conclusions for further work

We are responsible for creating the right medium in which to grow and give the best of ourselves.

If we know how to value different emotions and ways of seeing the world, and learn to care for this diversity, we will be stronger.

Not everything is valid. The diversity we value is based on respect for life, for people, for human rights, and the search for balance and emotional health.

OUR DIFFERENCE MAKES US STRONG

✹ Objective:

To realize that everyone has a mission in life and that comparison with others is not fair to ourselves.

Story:

There was once a beautiful garden with apple, orange, and pear trees and the most lovely rose bushes, but one of the trees was deeply sad because it had a problem: it didn't know who it was.

"What you need is concentration. If you really try, you'll be able to produce succulent apples. It's very easy," the apple tree told it.

"Don't listen to him. It's easier to make roses, and they're prettier than apples," the rose bush said.

Desperate, the poor tree tried to be everything the others said it should be, but it didn't succeed and felt increasingly frustrated.

One day an owl visited the garden and, seeing the tree's despair, said:

"Don't worry, your problem's not so serious. It's the same problem that many other beings on Earth have. Don't spend your energy on trying to be as others want you to be. Be yourself, know yourself, and listen to your inner voice."

And so the tree learned it would never produce apples because it wasn't an apple tree, but an oak. Its destiny was to grow tall and majestic, shelter birds, and give shade to travelers and beauty to the countryside. At last it felt strong and self-confident, and was admired and respected.

✹ Reflections on the story

- What is best: an apple tree, a rose bush, or an oak? Is it fair to compare them?

- How did the tree feel when it wanted to be what it wasn't? Why did it pay so much attention to the apple tree and the rose bush?

- Has anyone ever asked you to do things beyond your capacity?

- Are you sometimes compared with other people? How do you feel when this happens?

- Are you always waiting to hear what others think about you?

- What do you think of yourself?

- Can you think of three characteristics that define you?

✹ Conclusions for further work

Uniformity impoverishes us. A forest in which a wide variety of species coexist is richer and has a greater chance of survival than one containing just one species.

Differences stimulate us, fend off boredom, and allow us to learn from each other. We do not feel the same, and there's no need to do so. In the same situation, one person may feel anger, and another fear; one might consider an obstacle impossible to overcome, while another might think it a challenge; one person may feel confidence in a situation, and another anxiety. What we feel is not as important as what we do, and how we behave when we feel it.

The important thing is to give the best of ourselves, helping to improve everything around us.

CAMPAIGN TO RAISE AWARENESS

Objective:

To realize how important it is to care for emotional species to keep them from becoming extinct.

Activity:

Each group of children imagines that they are publicists asked to create an advertising campaign for certain emotions, encouraging people to behave in particular ways that spread these emotions widely. Each team spends a month preparing a campaign for one particular emotion: gratitude, joy, tenderness, peace, friendship.

First, they will research the emotional species they are promoting – where it grows best, the climate it likes, the vitamins that make it flourish, the benefits for everyone, etc.

Second, each team will design a publicity campaign using posters, T-shirts, and murals; playing particular songs; or recording excerpts from films that exemplify the emotion. Be as creative as possible!

Third, each group is asked to suggest simple, concrete behaviors for anyone who wants to participate daily in the campaign. Those who want to join must sign a contract promising to practice the behaviors for two weeks.

Then the groups share results and conclusions.

Reflections on the activity

- What is the most important thing you learned about the different emotions and feelings?

- How did you feel when working together to publicize your emotional species and foster its growth?

- Which part of the campaign was the hardest? Did you ask for help? Who from?

- Do you feel satisfied with the results?

- Did you take part in the campaign of your colleagues by acquiring a commitment to improve some aspect of your behavior?

Conclusions for further work

We can all work together to help valuable emotional species grow and develop. For gratitude, joy, tenderness, and friendship to grow, we need to create the right conditions. These species cannot grow in emotionally polluted areas or in small places that suffocate them. They need spaces of respect, freedom, responsibility, communication, sincerity, knowledge, and honesty.

Wishes are just smoke if they aren't transformed into concrete action. It is essential that reason and emotion work together. What would happen if a gardener did not water the seeds or fertilize the soil? Singing to plants is not enough; we have to take responsibility for looking after them. The same applies to people, doesn't it?

THE AUTHORS

Maria Mercè Conangla and **Jaume Soler** are psychologists and creators of Fundació Àmbit (Institute for Personal Growth), Barcelona, a nonprofit organization that since 1996 has provided training, counseling, and resources for personal growth and emotional education and management. Two of its most innovative offerings are the *ÀMBIT universit@rtdelviure* and the *master's in emotional ecology degree program*, which the authors co-direct. In 2002, their research and work in humanist psychology inspired them to create the new concept of emotional ecology, which they've developed in more than eleven books. The authors give frequent talks and teach master's-level courses at the University of Barcelona.

www.ecologiaemocional.org | www.fundacioambit.org

Other Schiffer Books by the Author:
Feelings Forecasters: A Creative Approach to Managing Emotions,
ISBN: 978-0-7643-5624-7
Relationship Navigators: A Creative Approach to Managing Emotions,
ISBN: 978-0-7643-5555-4

Other Schiffer Books on Related Subjects:
Unraveling Rose by Brian Wray,
ISBN: 978-0-7643-5393-2
Meditative Zendoodles: A Treasure Trove of Relaxing Moments by Susanne Schaadt,
ISBN: 978-0-7643-5289-8

Copyright © 2018 by Schiffer Publishing

Originally published as *Exploradores Emocionales* by Maria Mercè Conangla and Jaume Soler

Illustrations by Paloma Valdivia
©2013 ParramónPaidotribo
Badalona, Spain

Translated from the Spanish by
Ian Hayden Jones
Library of Congress Control Number: 2018937048

"Schiffer," "Schiffer Publishing, Ltd.," and the pen and inkwell logo are registered trademarks of Schiffer Publishing, Ltd.

Designed by: Jack Chappell
Cover Design by: Molly Shields
Editorial Direction: María Fernanda Canal
Illustrations: Paloma Valdivia
Edition: Cristina Vilella
Type set in: Stereofidelic/Jivetalk/Freehand575/Interstate

ISBN: 978-0-7643-5553-0
Printed in China

Published by Schiffer Publishing, Ltd.
4880 Lower Valley Road
Atglen, PA 19310
Phone: (610) 593-1777; Fax: (610) 593-2002
E-mail: Info@schifferbooks.com
Web: www.schifferbooks.com

For our complete selection of fine books on this and related subjects, please visit our website at www.schifferbooks.com. You may also write for a free catalog.

Schiffer Publishing's titles are available at special discounts for bulk purchases for sales promotions or premiums. Special editions, including personalized covers, corporate imprints, and excerpts, can be created in large quantities for special needs. For more information, contact the publisher.

We are always looking for people to write books on new and related subjects. If you have an idea for a book, please contact us at proposals@schifferbooks.com.